Star Friends

MOONLIGHT MISCHIEF

For Olivia Perkes,
who would be a perfect Star Friend,
and for the lovely Sandra Jimminson for all her
help—and that pitchfork suggestion! – L.C.

tiger tales

5 River Road, Suite 128, Wilton, CT 06897
Published in the United States 2022
Originally published in Great Britain 2019
by the Little Tiger Group
Text copyright © 2019 Linda Chapman
Illustrations copyright © 2019 Lucy Fleming and Mike Love
ISBN-13: 978-1-6643-4013-8
ISBN-10: 1-6643-4013-0
Printed in China
STP/1800/0431/0921
2 4 6 8 10 9 7 5 3 1

www.tigertalesbooks.com

18/24
CM

£2
CHI

Star Friends

Moonlight Mischief

BY LINDA CHAPMAN

ILLUSTRATED BY LUCY FLEMING

tiger tales

Contents

1
IN THE STAR WORLD

The hills and valleys were coated with stardust, and the trees in the forest glittered and shone. A silver wolf stood beside a peaceful forest pool with a large owl perched on her back. They were watching a picture on the surface of the water. The image was dark around the edges, but in the center they could see a girl with blond hair snuggled up in bed, holding a fox cub in her arms. The fox opened his indigo eyes and began licking the girl's nose. She woke up and giggled.

"Mia and Bracken," said the owl softly.

"They love each other very much indeed," said the wolf. A wistful look crossed her face. "I wish Mia's grandmother could have seen them together. She would have been so happy to know that her granddaughter had become a Star Friend—just like she did when she was younger."

"I hope Mia, Bracken, and their friends do as much good as her grandmother and you did, Silver," said the owl.

The wolf nodded. "I am sure they will. Since the girls became Star Friends, they have done an excellent job of keeping the town of Westport safe."

Every so often, animals from the magical Star World would travel down to the human world to find a girl or boy to be their Star Friend. They taught them how to connect with the magical current that ran between the two worlds. When a child became a Star

Friend, they and their animal bonded for life, using magic to do good—helping people around them to be happy and stopping anyone from using dark magic.

"Do you see the black cloud at the edge of the image?" said the owl. "It looks like dark magic is coming to Westport again."

"Mia and her friends will be ready for it," declared the wolf as they watched Mia throw back her comforter and jump out of bed, with Bracken bounding happily around her legs.

The owl hooted. "I hope so. Let us watch and see."

2
A Strange Vision

Mia giggled. "Try again, Bracken! Try harder!"

She was sitting on the floor with a magical silvery bubble surrounding her like a dome. Bracken leaped at it, but he simply bounced off it, landing on Mia's bedroom rug. He jumped back up and scratched at the sides with his paws. The dome wobbled slightly but didn't break.

Giving up, he sank back down on his haunches. "You're getting really good at making magic shields, Mia," he said, panting. "I can't get through at all."

Mia grinned and disconnected from the
magic current—it was like flicking a switch off
in her mind. The tingling buzz of magic slowly
faded from her blood, and the bubble vanished.
Bracken bounded forward and sprang onto
her lap. She wrapped her arms around him,
burying her face in his soft, russet-red fur.
She loved him so much. She'd only been a
Star Friend for six months, but already she
could hardly remember life before Bracken
and magic.

"It's really fun being able to make shields,"

she said. "And it might be useful if we have to fight another Shade."

Shades were evil spirits conjured by people using dark magic. They brought misery and chaos. Star Friends, like Mia, had to use magic to stop them and send them back to the Shadows where they belonged.

"Why don't you use your seeing magic to find out if there is anything we should be investigating at the moment?" said Bracken.

"Okay." Mia jumped to her feet and picked up a small mirror from her desk. Cupping it in her hands, she sat back down and gazed into the shining surface, opening herself to the current again. It tingled and sparked through her, like faint pins and needles in every cell of her body. Star Friends all had different magical abilities, and Mia was able to use the magic to look into the past and future, to see things that were happening elsewhere, and to get warnings from the magic if danger was coming. "Show me if there's anything we should be worried about," she whispered.

Her reflection faded in the glass, and a new image appeared. It showed the main road that led into the town of Westport—where Mia and her friends lived. The image dissolved and was replaced by a different picture—a cluster of houses, one covered in ivy that looked vaguely familiar. It quickly changed again, this time showing the back of a woman with short brown hair who was examining her reflection in a mirror with lights around it. There was something odd about the reflection—something that didn't seem quite right—but before Mia could figure out what it was, the image changed once more, and she caught a glimpse of a small black shape—a phone, or maybe a TV remote? Mia blinked in surprise. Why was the magic showing her a TV remote? But before she could look more closely, the surface of the mirror cleared, and all she saw was her own reflection again.

Mia told Bracken what she had seen. "I don't know what the pictures mean. I didn't see anything really scary, like a Shade or someone doing dark magic. Just a road, a woman, something that looked like a remote control, and some houses."

Bracken scratched his nose with a front paw. "The magic showed you those things for a reason. I wonder why."

Unease prickled through Mia. "I'd better tell the others so we can keep an eye out in case anything strange starts to happen."

Her best friends, Lexi, Sita, and Violet, were all Star Friends, too. They each had their own

Star Animal—Violet's was a wildcat named
Sorrel, Lexi's was a red squirrel named Juniper,
and Sita's was a gentle fallow deer named
Willow.

"Are we meeting up after school today?"
Bracken asked.

"Yes. Violet's asked us all over to her house
for dinner, but we'll go to the clearing first,"
said Mia.

The clearing was in the woods near Violet's
house. The girls often went there because it
was a beautiful place, full of very powerful
magic. Hardly anyone else ever visited the
clearing, which meant it was a safe spot where
they could practice magic with their animals.
The Star Animals tried not to be seen by other
humans—the Star World had to be kept secret
from anyone who wasn't a Star Friend.

"Mia! Breakfast!" her mom called from the
kitchen.

"Coming, Mom! I'll just get dressed!

I'd better go," she told Bracken, pulling on her school clothes. She gave him a quick hug. "I'll see you later."

"I'll miss you," Bracken said, licking her cheek. "Meet me as soon as you can."

"I will." Mia kissed his fluffy head and went downstairs.

Mia's two-year-old brother, Alex, was in the kitchen in his high chair, and her 15-year-old sister, Cleo, was sitting at the table, eating a piece of toast and flicking through a magazine. Her dad was trying to feed Alex oatmeal.

"Watch out!" he warned as Alex grabbed the spoon and waved it around, sending globs of oatmeal flying through the air. Mia ducked just in time.

"No, Alex, don't do that," said Mr. Greene. Alex chuckled and hit him on the head with his plastic spoon.

Mia bit back a grin. She knew she shouldn't giggle when Alex was being naughty, but sometimes it was very hard not to.

"So what's happening at school today?" her dad asked as Mia poured herself some cereal.

"Not much. Just spelling and times-tables tests."

"Lucky you," said Cleo, looking up enviously. "I've got precalculus, physics, and French. I wish I were still in fifth grade."

"Miss Harris also said Lexi, Violet, Sita, and I could help with some gardening at lunchtime," said Mia. "The flower bed by the kindergarten classroom is full of weeds, and we're going to clear it so the kindergarteners can plant some summer flowers there."

"Then remember to put sunscreen on before you go to school, and take a hat," said her dad. "It's supposed to be very warm today."

Mia glanced out the window at the blue sky. The last week had been very sunny. It was great now that the weather was getting warmer and the days stayed lighter longer—it made it much easier for her and the others to meet up after school.

"I can't wait for spring break," said Mia.

"What are you two going to do with all that free time?" her dad said.

"See friends and sleep!" Cleo yawned.

Mia listed her plans. "Sleepovers, swimming, maybe go to the movies, get ice cream from the Copper Kettle...."

She smiled to herself as she added in her head, *And do a lot of magic, too, of course!*

3
PRETTIEST SMALL TOWN COMPETITION

"I like gardening," said Sita happily.

"This bed is going to look so much better with flowers in it." It was lunchtime, and she, Mia, Violet, and Lexi were kneeling on mats by the flower bed in a quiet spot outside the kindergarten classroom, pulling up weeds and turning the soil over.

"It's so hot," said Lexi, pushing back her dark curls and fanning her face.

"It's the hottest day of the year so far," Violet informed them. "In fact, this is the hottest March on record." She sat back on her heels. "The average temperature in Westport has been—Ow!" She broke off as a thorn in the soil caught her wrist above the top of her gloves and scratched her skin. "That hurt!" she said, shaking her wrist and looking at the droplets of blood blooming in a line on her skin.

"Here," said Sita quickly. Reaching over, she took Violet's wrist in her hands and shut her eyes. She breathed in and out slowly.

The blood on Violet's pale skin vanished, and the scratch healed to a pink line that gradually faded away completely. Sita opened her eyes. "Better?"

"Much," said Violet. "Thank you."

"Your magic is awesome," Lexi told Sita.

Like Mia, the other girls could use the magic current to do different things. As well as healing, Sita had the ability to command people to do as she said, although she didn't like that power and only used it when she really had to. Lexi could run fast and be very agile. Violet could shadow-travel and disguise things, and she was also a Spirit Speaker, which meant that she could send Shades back to the Shadows where they belonged.

"I can't wait to meet up with the animals and do some magic together later," said Lexi. "I'm so glad I have an afternoon with no activities for once."

Lexi did a bunch of things after school and on the weekend—gymnastics, piano, flute, tennis, and French—which made it difficult for her to meet up with the others.

"How come you have tonight off?"

Mia asked her.

"Mom is letting me stop my extra math lessons now that I've passed the entrance exam for high school," Lexi said.

"It's going to be strange being at different schools in September," said Sita. "We'll be at Oceanview Middle School, and you'll be at Seaside High School."

"You'll all stay friends with me, won't you?" Lexi asked anxiously.

"Of course not," Mia teased. "We can't possibly be friends with you if you're at a different school."

But Lexi didn't smile as Mia had expected. She bit her lip and looked down at her hands.

"I didn't mean it," Mia said quickly. She hadn't for one second thought Lexi might take her seriously. "Of course we'll stay friends."

"So, if you're not doing math lessons now, does that mean you'll have every Monday night free?" Violet said, not seeming to notice that

Lexi was looking upset.

Lexi shrugged. "No such luck. It's just this week. I'm starting Spanish lessons next week."

"But you already speak German, what with your dad being German, *and* you're learning French," said Violet.

"I know, but apparently—" Lexi mimicked her mom's voice—"*learning a new language is so much easier when you're younger.* I can hardly say I want Mondays off so I can go and do magic." She sighed. "I wish I didn't have to do so many activities and I could meet up with you more."

"At least we have spring break coming up," said Sita. "That'll give us a lot of extra time together."

"A lot of time to use magic to do good and help people!" Mia said.

"And maybe fight Shades," said Violet, her green eyes sparkling.

Sita shuddered. "I don't know why you sound so excited about that! I'd be happy if I never saw a Shade ever again."

There were different types of Shades, but they all liked to make people unhappy and miserable—either by talking to them and twisting their thoughts, or by making bad things happen. Mia and the others had had to fight quite a few Shades since they had become Star Friends. Bad people had used dark magic to trap Shades in everyday objects like mirrors or toys so that they could get them into other people's houses.

"Do you remember those last Shades? he ones in the dreamcatchers that made all of the grown-ups they affected become really competitive?" said Mia. She pictured the Shades they had released from the dreamcatchers— tall, thin, and shadowy, with spiny fingers and glowing red eyes.

"And there was that one trapped in the garden gnome," said Sita. "The Wish Shade. Do you remember how he locked me and

Lexi in a shed and set fire to it? We could have burned to death! They're so dangerous!"

"*Shhh,*" Violet said quickly as Lucia, one of the kindergarten children, skipped over to them.

"Mia!" the little girl squealed, throwing her arms around Mia's waist. "I've been looking for you!" At Westport Elementary School, the kindergarteners were all assigned a Book Buddy from fifth grade. Mia was Lucia's Book Buddy.

"Hi, Lucia," said Mia, hugging her back.

"What are you doing?" asked Lucia as she wriggled free from the hug.

"Cleaning out this flower bed so your class can plant some flowers in it and it'll look pretty again," said Mia.

Lucia beamed. "Nana and Grandpa will be happy! They said we have to make the school look as nice as possible so Westport wins the prize in the town competition. Nana's coming into our assembly to talk to everyone about it this afternoon."

"Lucia's nana is Ana-Lucia Jefferson—the assistant principal," Mia explained to the others.

Understanding dawned on their faces. They usually saw Ana-Lucia, or Mrs. Jefferson as she was called, around the school. She often visited the classes during the day to listen to the children reading. She was always very smiley and friendly. Mike, her husband, who had lived in the town all his life, was part of the Parent Teacher Student Association, and was involved with many different fundraising events.

"What's the competition for?" Violet said. She liked any kind of competition.

"It's for the Prettiest Small Town," said Sita. "My dad was telling me about it. All the small towns can enter. Westport won it a few years ago."

"Nana and Grandpa really want Westport to win again this year," said Lucia. "They're moving to Portugal after the summer when Nana retires. Grandpa said he would really love to see Westport win once more before they go."

"Maybe we can help clean up the town," said Lexi.

"That's what Nana's going to talk about in the assembly," said Lucia. She threw her arms wide. "She wants *everyone* to help."

The bell rang on the playground.

"Time to pack up," said Sita.

Lucia ran off to line up with her class while Mia and the others put the gardening equipment away in the shed and hurried inside to wash their hands.

"So, if all of you could help Westport try and win the Prettiest Small Town competition, it would be absolutely fantastic!" Mrs. Jefferson said as she finished her talk in assembly.

Lucia's nana had dark brown, sleek, chin-length hair with some strands of silvery gray. Her voice had a faint accent—she had lived in Westport for many years but had grown up in Portugal.

"The competition is being judged next week. We need yards to be cleaned up, litter to be picked up, the school to look spick and span. If everyone joins in and works together, I'm sure we can manage it. Can I count on you all to help?"

Everyone nodded.

"It's a great idea," said Mrs. King, the

principal, standing up. "Why don't all of the classes use the time between now and the end of school to think about what they can do?"

The assembly ended, and for the rest of the afternoon, the two fifth-grade classes made posters to put up around town telling people about the competition and asking them to keep everything looking clean.

Mia really enjoyed designing her poster, although at the table next to her, some of the more annoying boys in her class—Dan, Nikhil, and Josh—were moaning.

"This is so boring," Dan said.

"Yeah, who wants to make posters for some silly contest," agreed Josh, putting his pen down.

"I'm not cleaning up the town," said Nikhil, abandoning his poster and sticking his arms behind his head.

"Come on, boys," said Miss Harris, walking over. "Get going with your posters."

They reluctantly picked up their pens again, but as she walked off, Mia heard them muttering together again.

"Silly contest."

Everyone else, however, seemed eager to finish their posters and make plans to help. The afternoon passed quickly, and Mia was almost sad when school finished—but then she remembered that she and the others were going to the clearing to meet up with the animals and do magic!

It was wonderful to leave the stuffy classroom and get out into the fresh air. Violet turned her face to the sun. "Let's ask my dad if we can get ice cream from the Copper Kettle on the way home. It's definitely an ice-cream day."

"Every day should be an ice-cream day," Mia declared. Mary, who ran the Copper Kettle café, made the best homemade ice cream ever!

They ran over to where Violet's dad was talking to Ana and Mike Jefferson, a tall, slim,

balding man who had an air of energy and
enthusiasm about him. Lucia was with them.
She had an old red shoebox in her arms.

"It's the PTSA fortune-telling evening
tonight," Mr. Jefferson was saying to Violet's
dad. "Are you coming?"

Violet's dad chuckled. "It's not my cup of tea.
You don't really believe in things like that, do
you, Mike?"

"Oh, he does," said his wife, shaking her head
affectionately at her husband. "The horoscopes
are the first thing he looks at it in the paper
every morning."

"You may laugh, but I believe that it's good to keep an open mind." Mr. Jefferson smiled. "Maybe this fortune teller really can see into the future." He turned to Mia. "Your mom's coming, isn't she, Mia?"

Mia nodded.

"Lucia's staying over with us tonight," said Mrs. Jefferson. "So if you'd like to come over, Mia, please do. Lucia would love to have someone to play with while the fortune-telling is going on."

"Come over, Mia. *Pleeease!*" begged Lucia.

"Okay," Mia said. "I'm going to Violet's house now, but I'll come over with Mom later."

As Violet started to ask her dad if they could stop at the Copper Kettle, Lucia showed the box she was holding to Mia. "Look what I brought in for show-and-tell today!"

She opened the lid to reveal two large dolls with dark hair—a man and a woman.

The female doll was wearing a heavy black skirt over a white shirt with puffy sleeves and black plastic oval-shaped shoes, and she had a basket of plastic fruit on her head. The male doll was a shepherd with a red waistcoat, black knee-length pants, a green hat like an elf's, and a wooden shepherd's crook in his hands.

"They're Nana's. Do you like them?" asked Lucia.

Mia didn't really like dolls much, and these two had creepy glass eyes that blinked as Lucia moved the box. However, she didn't want to be rude. "They're … um … beautiful."

"When I was little, I used to collect dolls in traditional dress from different countries," said Mrs. Jefferson. "My father used to travel a lot, and he would buy them for me. These were my first two dolls—they're Portuguese."

"Like you, Nana," said Lucia.

Her nana smiled. "Yes, just like me."

"It's not long until you move to Portugal, is it?" Violet's dad said.

"No, the end of the summer," said Mr. Jefferson. "I've been practicing my Portuguese. Luckily, it's pretty similar to Spanish, and I'm fluent in that."

Just then, Lexi and Sita came hurrying out of their classroom—they were in a different fifth-grade class than Mia and Violet. "Sorry we're late. We were just finishing our posters," said Sita.

"Can we walk home past the Copper Kettle, Dad?" Violet asked. "It's such a nice day—perfect for ice cream!"

"Well, I have the car, but you can walk if you want to, and I'll meet you at home. Here's some money for ice cream."

"Thank you!" the girls chorused.

"See you later, Lucia," Mia called as she set off with the others. It was time for some magic—and fun!

4
AFTERNOON MAGIC

As the girls walked through Westport's pretty winding streets, past the village green and duck pond, they saw a few of the older members of the town out and about, weeding the churchyard and planting flowers around the edge of the village green. The sun seemed to be making everyone cheerful, and people smiled at them and said hello as they passed.

"Everyone's really getting involved with cleaning up, aren't they?" said Lexi. "We should offer to help this weekend."

"We could use magic!" Violet suggested.

"But I don't see how any of our magic powers can help," said Mia.

Violet's green eyes sparkled. She cast a quick look around, and then stared at an old bench near them. It changed from shabby-looking to brand-new.

"Violet, stop it!" Lexi hissed in alarm. "Someone might see!"

Violet grinned, and the illusion faded. "Don't worry, Miss Sensible. No one was watching."

Mia saw Lexi's mouth tighten.

"It's a shame that my magic only lasts for as long as I'm concentrating on the illusion," Violet went on. "So it's no use for the competition. But you could use your magic, Lexi. You could climb onto roofs and get rid of any moss and take plastic bags out of the trees and—"

"What if someone saw Lexi? Maybe we

should just help without magic," Sita interrupted.

"I guess," Violet agreed reluctantly. "But using magic is so much more fun!"

They continued down the street. Sita and Violet chatted about how they could use magic if only they didn't have to keep it secret, but Mia noticed that Lexi was walking a little way behind them.

"Are you okay?" she said, falling back and linking arms with her. Lexi nodded but didn't say anything.

They reached the Copper Kettle café. The door was open, and Mary, the cheerful owner, was standing behind the counter with her assistant Rebecca. "Afternoon, girls! What can I get you? Ice cream, I'm guessing?"

"Yes, please!" they chorused, crowding around the ice-cream counter. The different flavors of ice cream looked as colorful as a rainbow.

"Dad gave me enough money for us all to get two scoops," Violet said.

"Could I have strawberry and mint chocolate chip, please?" said Mia.

Mary took a cone and started scooping the ice cream. "You really do make the best ice cream," Mia told her.

"I have a secret recipe my Cornish grandmother gave me," Mary said with a smile. "Everyone always said she used magic because it tasted so good!"

"I bet you've been selling a lot with it being so sunny," Lexi said.

"Actually, I haven't," Mary said. "It's because of that new water-sports center that just opened farther down the coast. I guess people are going there instead. I'm hoping things pick up during spring break. It's been much quieter here than it usually is at this time of year."

"If Westport wins the Prettiest Small Town competition, that might help," said Violet.

Mary nodded. "I'm hoping so. I've cleaned up the front of the store and put out hanging baskets, and I'm going to help clean up the area around the duck pond this weekend. The grass is very overgrown there. The fence around the baseball field needs repainting, too. Mr. Jefferson asked me to help; he seems eager to get everyone involved."

"Lucia said he really wants us to win this competition," said Mia.

"Well, I hope we do, too," said Mary. She handed Mia her ice cream and then made cones for Lexi and Violet. Sita simply couldn't choose—she was hopeless at making decisions—so in the end, the others chose for her.

They headed across the main street. On one side was the town, and on the other side were woods and the ocean. They walked down the small, stony road that led through the trees to the beach, quickly eating their ice-cream cones before they melted. Violet's house was at the end of the road, but they didn't stop. They just dumped their school bags in the yard, waved to Violet's dad, and hurried on. They wanted to get to the clearing to see the animals!

Just opposite the path that led to the clearing was a pretty house where Mia's grandmother had lived before she died. Mia always felt a flicker of sadness when she looked at it. She really missed her grandmother, but being a Star Friend helped because the magic had shown her that her grandmother had been a Star Friend, too. Her animal had been a beautiful silver wolf.

"I'm glad Elizabeth is gone," said Violet,

stopping to look at the house. A lady named Elizabeth had bought it at Christmastime, but she had been doing some very dark magic. The girls had managed to stop her and get her to leave before she caused too much damage. Now the house was for sale again, but no one had bought it yet.

"I hope the next person who buys it is normal and nice!" said Mia.

"Come on, you two," said Lexi impatiently, climbing up the small bank and onto the path that led to the clearing. It got very overgrown with Queen Anne's lace later in the summer, but at this time of year, it was easy to walk down. It twisted and turned through the trees before coming out in the hidden clearing where Mia had first met Bracken.

A stream danced over a small waterfall and headed on merrily through the trees to join the ocean. The leaves on the trees were thick and green, and spring daffodils had given way to bluebells and thick clumps of pink-flowered campion that clustered around the tree trunks. Birds sang, and squirrels scampered along the branches.

The girls called their animals' names.

"Sorrel!"

"Bracken!"

"Willow!"

"Juniper!"

The Star Animals appeared instantly. Bracken took a flying leap into Mia's arms and nuzzled her neck with his cold black nose. Juniper leaped onto Lexi's shoulder, playing with her hair with his tiny paws and chattering softly. Sorrel twined herself through Violet's legs, purring loudly, while Willow rubbed her forehead against Sita.

In that moment, Mia felt so happy that she wouldn't have wanted to be anywhere else in the world.

"Is it magic time?" Bracken said eagerly.

"Yep," Mia said, hugging him.

He jumped down and bounced around her legs in excitement, almost knocking Sorrel over. She hissed in annoyance. "Why do you have to be so clumsy, fox?"

"Whoops! Sorry, cat!" he said, not looking sorry at all.

Sorrel stalked away. "Violet, show the others what you've been practicing at home." She sat down at a safe distance from Bracken and flicked her tabby tail around her paws.

"Okay," said Violet. "Watch this." She shut her eyes. The air around her seemed to shimmer, and then suddenly, she wasn't there anymore. Instead, they were looking at Mrs. King, their principal!

"Oh … my…. Wow!" gasped Mia.

Sorrel looked smug. "It's good, isn't it?"

"It's amazing," said Sita.

Lexi nodded. "I thought you could only disguise other things. I didn't realize you could disguise yourself to look like another person."

"I only discovered I could the other day," said Violet. Mia blinked. It was really odd seeing Mrs. King standing there but hearing Violet's voice coming out of her mouth. "At first, I could only manage to change part of me into someone else, but I've been practicing, and I've gotten better at it. Now I just need to learn how to disguise my voice." She transformed back into herself. "It could be really useful if we ever need to spy on someone."

"Violet's so clever," purred Sorrel. Violet tickled her under the chin, and Sorrel purred again.

"Mia's clever, too!" said Bracken quickly. "Come on, Mia, show the others how good your shields are getting!"

So Mia opened herself to the current and conjured a shield around herself. The silvery bubble shimmered in the sunlight. Lexi threw pine cones at it, and Willow butted it while

Juniper scampered up it and bounced up and down on the top, but the shield held firm.

"See? Mia's amazing, too," said Bracken as Juniper jumped off with a flick of his bushy red tail, and Mia let the shield fade.

Lexi sighed. "I wish I could do some other kind of magic. Everyone but me has extra powers."

"But being really agile is incredible," said Sita.

"Mmm," said Lexi, not looking convinced.

"Yeah, I wish I could run as fast as you," said Mia.

Juniper scampered up Lexi's leg and onto her shoulder. "Your powers are amazing, Lexi." He rubbed her cheek with his paw. "I think they're the best."

Lexi gave a small smile. "Thanks, Juniper." He swung himself into her arms and she cuddled him, hiding her face in his fur.

Mia frowned. For a few weeks now, she'd

had the feeling that something was bothering Lexi. She'd seemed a lot quieter than usual.

"How about we play tag?" said Sita quickly. "Us three against you, Lexi. You're too quick for us to play any other way."

"Okay," said Lexi, her eyes lighting up with some of their usual sparkle. "Catch me if you can!" She raced to the other side of the clearing. The others and their animals charged after her, but Lexi could duck and dive and swerve faster than anyone.

They played tag until they were all exhausted and then practiced their magic some more—Sita repairing some bluebells that had been damaged in the game, Lexi practicing her climbing, and Violet moving around the clearing, using the shadows to appear and disappear. Mia remembered what she had seen that morning in her mirror, and once again tried asking the magic to show her if there was anything they should be worried about.

The same four images fleeted across the surface of her pocket mirror. They didn't make any more sense now than they had then.

"What are you seeing?" Violet asked, appearing beside her and making her jump. The others came over and listened, too, as Mia explained.

"I wonder what the magic is trying to warn us about," Mia finished.

"It doesn't sound like it's anything too scary," said Sita hopefully. "A woman looking at herself in a mirror, the main street leading into Westport outside the Copper Kettle, some houses, and a TV remote."

"Maybe it's showing the street because it's trying to tell us that someone is coming to Westport," said Violet thoughtfully. "Someone who's going to cause trouble."

Sorrel purred. "Very good thinking, Violet."

Mia put her mirror back in her pocket. "Well, if something is coming, we'll deal with it like we always do," she declared. "We're Star Friends, and anyone who's planning on doing dark magic in Westport had better watch out!"

5
MYSTIC MAUREEN

When Mia arrived home, she changed her clothes to go with her mom to Mr. and Mrs. Jefferson's house.

"Promise me you won't listen if that fortune teller says we're going to move the family to Antarctica!" Mia's dad said to her mom as they left.

Mia's mom chuckled. "All right, but can I believe her if she sees great wealth and happiness in our future?"

"Yep, that's fine—you can believe that," said

Mia's dad, kissing her and ruffling Mia's hair. "See you both later. Have a good evening."

They got into the car.

"Do you believe in fortune-telling, Mom?" Mia asked as they drove through the town.

"No," her mom said. "It's just for fun. No one can see the future, Mia."

But Mia knew that that wasn't true, because *she* could. Not all of it, and not always very clearly, but she could see some things. A thought jumped into her mind. Maybe this fortune teller was a Star Friend and really *could* see the future. Or maybe she used a different type of magic, like crystal magic or plant magic, to predict things. Mia felt very curious to meet her.

Ana and Mike Jefferson lived near to the school in a pretty house with a very neat front yard; there were flowers all the way around, and a new birdbath. The house next door to theirs looked very unkempt in comparison—it had ivy scrambling across the walls, a yard that was

overgrown with weeds, and large clumps of
moss on the roof tiles. Mia frowned, feeling that
a memory was trying to push itself to the front
of her mind. *Ivy....*

But just then, she was distracted by the sound
of laughing as Josh, Dan, and Nikhil came
racing down the street on their scooters and
started doing tricks.

As Mia's mom parked the car, the door of
the untidy house opened, and an elderly man
stomped out. "Will you boys get lost!" he
shouted angrily. "Go and ride those things
somewhere else. I'm trying to watch television!"

"Evening, Mr. Keating," said Mia's mom as the boys rolled their eyes and scootered away.

He went inside and shut his door with a bang.

"Mr. Keating really shouldn't have chosen to live close to a school if he doesn't like children playing," said Mia's mom. "The boys weren't doing anything wrong."

Mia followed her mom up Mr. and Mrs. Jefferson's neat path. Mr. Jefferson opened the door. "Hello, you two—come on in," he said.

"Mia!" cried Lucia, running out of the kitchen as Mia walked into the house.

"Why don't you show Mia around, Lucia?" Mr. Jefferson suggested. "Nicky, come and meet Mystic Maureen, our fortune teller. She's in the kitchen."

Lucia dragged Mia all over the house, showing her the large living room, and the study where the fortune teller was going to see people. There was a table covered with a purple shawl and a large crystal ball in the center. Mia felt a shiver run down her spine as she looked at it. They had once fought someone who used crystals to do dark magic. It had been very scary.

Next, Lucia took her into the dining room. "Look at all of Nana's dolls," she said, showing Mia a deep window ledge, which had a display of dolls from different countries. They were all shapes and sizes. Along with the two Portuguese dolls, there was a Spanish flamenco dancer in a red dress; a male German doll dressed in knee-length dungarees and carrying a blunt pitchfork; a female doll dressed as an Irish dancer; an American cheerleader holding an American flag; a male French doll with a large plastic baguette in his hands and a string of onions around his neck; and a female doll from Switzerland in an embroidered dress holding a milk churn.

Mia suppressed a shiver as she looked at the glassy eyes staring at her. Mia had always preferred cuddly animal toys to dolls when she was growing up. These dolls were particularly creepy with their old-fashioned clothes.

"Let's go get a drink," she said, turning away quickly.

She followed Lucia into the bright, spacious kitchen. Mr. Jefferson was taking some chicken wings out of the oven, while Mrs. Jefferson was arranging cookies on a plate.

A red-haired woman who Mia didn't know was standing by the sink. She had a floaty scarf around her neck and wore a long pink, orange, and blue dress, a bunch of bracelets, and a necklace made of multicolored beads that had a silver *M* hanging from it.

"Hi, Mia. This is Maureen, the fortune teller," said Mrs. Jefferson.

Maureen gave them a friendly smile. "Are you joining us this evening?"

"No, Mia's here to play with me," said Lucia.

"Are you sure you don't want your fortunes read?" Maureen's light brown eyes twinkled, and she pulled her scarf up over her head and suddenly spoke in a mysterious, spooky voice. "I am Mystic Maureen. I can look through the veils of the present and see into the future. Shall I tell you your fortunes, my dears?"

She took hold of Lucia's hand. "A-ha, what do I see here? Ice cream and beaches and swimming—"

"But I don't like swimming!" interrupted Lucia.

"I see you watching people swimming, then, and having a lot of fun!" She tickled Lucia's palm, making the little girl giggle and squirm away.

"And you, my dear." Her fingers closed over Mia's.

For a moment, Mia tensed. If Maureen really could do magic, maybe she would somehow see

Mia was a Star Friend!

"Ah, I spy a handsome boy in your future, and singing and dancing. I can see you like putting on makeup and going to parties." The fortune teller winked at Mia. "There are no secrets from Mystic Maureen!"

Mia relaxed. It was clear that Maureen had no magic at all. Mia never wore makeup, and she didn't go to the types of parties with music and boys. The only parties she liked usually involved things like swimming or bounce houses!

"Cookie, anyone?" Mrs. Jefferson asked, offering the plate around.

Maureen straightened up, pushing her scarf back. "Well, I won't say no," she said, speaking in her normal voice. She took a bite. "These are delicious!"

"My mother used to bake them for me when I was little," said Mrs. Jefferson. "It's an old Portuguese recipe."

"I'd love to have it," said Maureen.

"No problem. I have it written down—I can make a copy of it for you before you leave."

"I showed Mia your dolls, Nana," said Lucia, taking a cookie.

"Dolls?" said Maureen.

"I used to collect traditional dolls when I was little," Mrs. Jefferson explained.

"What a coincidence! I love dolls—I collect china ones," said Maureen. "I'd love to see your collection."

"Of course! They're in the dining room. Please take a look," Mrs. Jefferson said, showing her to the door. "We'd better get this food into the living room."

Mia and Lucia helped carry the food and drinks. People were going to be able to eat and chat there while they were waiting to see Mystic Maureen. When everything was set up, they went into the dining room. Maureen was taking a photo of the German doll.

"I'm sorry—I hope you don't mind," she

said to Mrs. Jefferson, moving the doll back to his position with the others and slipping her phone into her pocket. "I just had to take some photos. They're amazing."

"I don't mind at all," said Mrs. Jefferson, smiling. "It's wonderful to meet someone else who appreciates them."

"Well, I'd better get ready for my customers," said Maureen, pulling her scarf back over her head and setting off for the study.

There was a knock at the front door. "I'll get it!" called Mr. Jefferson.

"Let's go upstairs, Mia," said Lucia. "I want to show you the bedroom I stay in when I sleep over at Nana and Grandpa's. It has the bounciest bed ever!"

By the time the evening was over, Mia felt
worn out. She'd played game after game with
Lucia, helped her get ready for bed, and read
her five stories. The little girl had only just
fallen asleep when Mia's mom called upstairs.
"Time to go!"

"Thanks so much, Mia," said Mr. Jefferson
as she came downstairs. "It really helped
having you here to amuse Lucia."

"No problem," said Mia. She and her mom
said good-bye and left.

"So, did you have your fortune told?"
Mia asked her mom curiously. "What did
Mystic Maureen say?"

Mia's mom laughed. "Oh, nothing much.
She said I'm going to go traveling, and
someone named Raymond is very important
to me. But I don't know any Raymonds! It
was all very silly but good fun, and we raised a

decent amount of money for the school."
She stifled a yawn. "I'm tired now, though."

"Me, too," said Mia. "Taking care of a five year old is *very* hard work."

As soon as Mia was home, she got ready for bed. When her mom had said good night and turned off the overhead light, Mia called Bracken. He cuddled up to her, and she wrapped her arms around him. "It's been a busy day," she said, feeling her eyes starting to close.

He snuggled closer. "This is my favorite part of any day," he said.

Mia smiled sleepily and shut her eyes. "Mine, too," she whispered as she fell asleep.

6
Strange Happenings

"Mia! Wake up!" Mia felt her nose being licked and woke with a start, sitting bolt upright in bed.

"Are you okay?" Bracken asked. He was standing beside her, peering down at her anxiously. "You were tossing and turning and saying, 'Stay back! Go away!' Were you having a nightmare?"

Mia nodded. "It was about Mrs. Jefferson's dolls. She has this big collection of them." She shook her head and tried to clear the nightmare from her mind. "They were chasing me." She shuddered. "It was horrible."

"Do you think it was a magic dream?" Bracken asked anxiously. Although Mia had normal dreams like everyone else, she also had magic dreams, which warned her about dangers that were coming.

"I don't know.... No, I don't think so," she decided. "There were no Shades or people doing dark magic. It was probably just a regular bad dream—those dolls were creepy enough to give anyone nightmares."

She yawned and checked her clock. "It's almost morning." She glanced at the crack in her curtains and saw that it was getting light outside. "There's no point in going back to sleep."

She lay back, and Bracken stretched out on her chest. His whiskers tickled her cheek. "Can we meet and do more magic today?" he asked hopefully.

"We can, but Lexi won't be able to join us," said Mia. "She's always really busy on Tuesday nights." She rubbed his fur and sighed. "I hope Lexi is okay," she said.

"What do you mean?" asked Bracken.

"I don't know. She just seems a little quieter than usual. Like something's on her mind."

"Have you asked Sita or Violet if they've noticed anything?" Bracken asked.

Mia smiled. "Violet never notices anything."

Violet had many of good qualities, but being sensitive to others wasn't one of them, although she had been getting better at that since she'd become friends with Mia and the others.

"I'll ask Sita what she thinks. She's always really good at spotting when people are feeling down."

"I hope Lexi's all right," said Bracken.

Mia hugged him. "It may just be me imagining things. Anyway—" she changed the subject—"why don't I get up and see if the magic will show me anything else useful?" She was just pushing back her covers when her phone buzzed. She checked it and saw a message from Lexi.

> Are u all okay? I woke up during the night with a really weird feeling. I felt really scared, like something bad was about to happen. Lxx

Mia replied.

> I'm fine. Mxx

Her phone buzzed again with a message from Sita.

> Me, too. Sxxx

Almost immediately Violet joined in.

And me but OMG! Have u heard about the stuff that happened during the night? The grass around the pond has been cut, and the baseball-field fence has been painted! No one knows who did it! Isn't that WEIRD?! Vx

Mia gasped as she read the text.

"What is it?" said Bracken.

Mia read Violet's text out. "I wonder who did those things," she said. "And why at night?"

"It's really strange," said Bracken.

Lexi and Sita sent texts pinging back.

That's so odd! Sxx

Least it's not something terrible! Maybe someone's trying 2 help the town win the contest! Lxx

Mia added her thoughts.

A mystery that doesn't involve dark magic for once. Nice change! Mxx

She put her phone down. "Maybe we'll find out more about it at school."

On the way to school, Mia, her mom, and Alex took a detour to look at the baseball field. Mrs. Jefferson and Lucia were already there, peering at the fence.

"I had to come and take a look when Mike told me about it. I can't believe someone painted it during the night," said Mrs. Jefferson.

"And mowed the grass by the pond, too. How did no one see anything—or hear anything?" said Mia's mom as Alex wriggled to get out of his stroller. "It's like there's been a good fairy in town! Yes, you can get out for a minute, but don't run off, Alex," she said, undoing the buckles. "It's a real mystery. If they were mowing the lawn by the pond, it must have made a noise."

"But that's the strange thing. Mike said it looks like whoever did it cut the grass by hand with shears. And that's not all—they cleaned up

Mr. Keating's yard, too," said Mrs. Jefferson. "He was very shocked this morning. Mike says it must be someone who wants to help us win the Prettiest Small Town competition."

Mia's mom shot Mrs. Jefferson a look. "It wasn't Mike, was it?"

Mrs. Jefferson laughed. "Definitely not! I know he wants to win, but not enough to go creeping around in the dark, and he was definitely in bed beside me all night long."

Mia noticed Alex picking something up from the grass and lifting it to his mouth. "No, Alex," she said, running over and grabbing it. At first, she thought it was a bottle top. It was made of smooth black plastic and was about the right size, but it was oval-shaped rather than round. She didn't know what it was. She looked around for a garbage can but couldn't see one, so she shoved it in her coat pocket.

"Come on—let's get you in again, young man," said Mia's mom, lifting Alex back into his stroller. "We'd better get to school."

Lucia held Mia's hand as they walked along the sidewalk. "Who do you think did all those nice things, Mia?" Lucia asked.

"I don't know," said Mia, mystified. "I really don't have a clue."

Everyone at school was just as baffled. "It doesn't make sense," Violet said as she and the others walked around town later that morning. They had been allowed out to put up their posters with their teachers supervising them. "I mean, why would someone do all of those things at night? Why not just do them during the day? And why be so secretive?"

"I guess it was someone just trying to do

a good deed," said Sita. "We don't need to worry about it, though. After all, it's not like someone's been doing horrible things."

"I don't like mysteries," said Violet, frowning. "Hey, Mia, could you use your magic to see what happened last night?"

Mia pulled out her mirror from her pocket. "You three put up the posters in case Mr. Neal or Miss Harris comes along to check on what we're doing while I see what I can find out."

She cupped the mirror in her hand. As the magic current flowed into her, she whispered, "Show me what happened in Westport last night—show me the fence being painted." The surface of the mirror swirled, and an image of the baseball field appeared. Excitement bubbled up inside her. Was she about to solve the mystery and find out who painted the fence?

But she didn't see a person painting the fence—she saw a couple of shapes moving swiftly across the field, but they traveled so fast that they were just a blur, and then shadows swirled across the image, blocking the picture with darkness. "Oh!" she said in surprise.

"What did you see?" asked Violet.

"I didn't see anything, really, just shadows," Mia said slowly.

Sita's forehead wrinkled. "But I thought you only saw shadows when someone was using a spell to stop people from spying on them with magic."

Mia nodded. "I do."

There was silence as her words sank in.

"So the good deeds last night were done with magic?" said Violet.

"Not dark magic, though," said Sita anxiously. "It can't be. The things that happened were *nice*."

"Maybe someone is using magic for good," suggested Lexi. "Someone who doesn't want to be found out." She caught her breath, her eyes widening. "You don't think there could be another Star Friend in town, do you?"

"But wouldn't our animals know if there was?" said Violet. "Sorrel told me once that she could always tell if there were other Star Animals nearby."

"We need to talk to them," said Mia. Her mind was turning everything over. What was going on? Could someone else really be doing good magic in Westport?

"We'd better go to the clearing after school," said Violet.

"I can't," said Lexi. "I have gymnastics." She sighed. "But you three go. We need to find out what's going on."

"Okay, if you're sure," said Violet.

Lexi nodded. "I'm used to it."

"We'll tell you what the animals say," promised Sita.

"Girls!" They turned and saw Miss Harris waving to them from the end of the street. "Time to get back to school!"

"Coming!" they called.

They went back up the street and headed past the duck pond with the freshly-cut grass around it. It looked much neater, although the ducks were making a bit of a mess on it. Josh, Dan, and Nikhil were messing around, picking up grass with duck poop in it and throwing it at each other.

Mia saw their posters lying on the ground. "You still haven't put those up!"

"So?" said Dan, stuffing them in a nearby garbage can. "Who cares? Race you back to school!" he said to his friends, and they set off at a run.

"You know, I'm not sure putting the posters up was actually such a good idea," said Lexi, looking around at all the lampposts with posters flapping from them. "It makes everything look messy."

Mia knew what she meant. She had a feeling Mr. Jefferson would be taking the posters down before the actual judging! Still, it had been fun making them.

As Mia and the others got closer to school, they saw Mr. Keating standing in his front yard, talking across the fence to Mr. Jefferson. Mr. Keating did not look happy. "It's just not right—people coming into my yard at night," he grumbled, waving his hand at his front yard, which was looking much neater than it was the day before, with the flower beds weeded and raked over and the grass cut.

"I thought I heard something—strange whispering voices, and someone moving around. I should have come outside, but I was in bed. If I'd known what was going on, I'd have come right out and given those do-gooders a piece of my mind. They had no right to come into my yard!"

"It's a real mystery, but your yard does look better, John," Mr. Jefferson said.

Mr. Keating huffed. "Well, it's still not right," he muttered, shaking his head.

7
MORE ODD EVENTS

Mia, Violet, and Sita ran to the clearing
that afternoon and called their Star Animals.
Bracken, Sorrel, and Willow appeared
instantly. "We really need to talk to you!"
said Mia. "Strange stuff has been going on.
Last night...."

"Wait!" Willow tensed, her delicate ears
pricking. "Someone's coming through the
trees over there!"

The animals vanished in the blink of an eye.
The girls looked around. Hardly anyone

ever came to the clearing. They saw Mary
from the Copper Kettle walking through the
trees. "Hello, girls!" she said in surprise.

"Hi, Mary," said Mia.

"I'm just getting a
breath of fresh air.
I've been busy baking
cakes all afternoon.
I like walking in
the woods if I need
to clear my head,
and this clearing is
always so beautiful."
Mary smiled. "But
don't let me disturb
you. You carry on with
whatever you were doing."

"It's okay," said Mia. "We'll go down to the
beach."

They said good-bye and hurried away.
The path led to a small parking lot, and from

the parking lot, a track wound its way down the cliff to the beach. The tide was way out, and there weren't many people around.

"Let's go to our secret place," said Mia to the others.

At the base of the cliffs, there was a line of big boulders and rocks. In one particular spot, the girls had found a gap between some boulders. Through the gap there was a sheltered circle of pebbles where they could call their animals, shielded from sight by the large rocks. They squeezed through the gap and called their animals' names.

"Okay," said Mia as the three animals appeared. "Let's start again!"

"I don't understand this!" Sorrel stalked around Mia, Violet, and Sita after they'd finished explaining what had been going on. "I don't understand it at all."

"There can't be another Star Friend and Star Animal nearby," said Bracken.

"We'd definitely know if someone was using the magic current to do Star Magic," said Willow. "We'd feel it."

"So, it's not someone using Star Magic then," said Mia.

"No, but whoever it is must definitely be using some kind of magic if they're blocking you from seeing them," said Bracken.

Sorrel's indigo eyes were suspicious. "Whoever can do that must be able to do powerful magic. I don't like this at all."

"Me, neither," said Bracken. They looked at each other in surprise. They weren't used to agreeing.

"What should we do?" Sita asked them.

"There's nothing much we can do but wait and see what else happens," said Willow.

"Maybe nothing else *will* happen," Sita said hopefully. "Maybe it was just a one-time thing."

Sorrel sniffed. "Oh, no. Someone who can do such powerful magic is not going to just use it once, and maybe next time he or she won't use it for good."

Mia cuddled Bracken, a feeling of foreboding running down her spine.

When Mia walked to school with her dad and Alex the next day, they found that all of the posters that the fifth graders had put up the day before had been ripped down and stuffed into a garbage can.

"That's such a mean thing to do," said Mia, feeling upset.

Mia's dad nodded. "Who would do something so horrible?"

The other parents and grandparents they met on the way in were all asking the same questions, and as they got close to school, they saw a group of people gathered outside Mr. Keating's yard.

They joined the crowd and saw that all of the ivy that had been covering Mr. Keating's house had been cut down overnight. There wasn't a single leaf left in the yard, just the stumps of ivy stems at ground level. Mr. Keating was standing in his yard, looking furious. As Mia stared at the ivy on the ground, something stirred in her mind. A memory started to surface, but a shout interrupted her thoughts.

"Who did this? Who did it?" Mr. Keating ranted. He pointed at Josh, Dan, and Nikhil, who were standing near the fence, nudging each other and pointing. "Was it you three boys? Was it? You're always messing around outside my house."

"No!" Nikhil said quickly. "It wasn't us!"

"Why would we come and cut down your ivy?" Josh said in surprise.

Mr. Keating shook his fist at them. "If it was you boys, you'll be sorry!"

The boys hurried on to school. Alex started to cry in his stroller.

"Come on. We'd better get going," Mia's dad said.

Mia followed him. Her thoughts were racing. *Who would have cut down Mr. Keating's ivy and taken down all of the posters? And why?*

When she and her dad reached the school playground, they found all of the kindergarten children crying. Mia saw Dan, Nikhil, and Josh comforting their Book Buddies.

"What's going on?" Mia's dad said, going up to Mr. Jefferson and a sobbing Lucia.

Mr. Jefferson looked unhappy. "During the night, someone came and dug up the flowers that the kindergarteners planted yesterday."

"No!" exclaimed Mia. She'd seen the flower bed the day before, after the kindergarteners had been out planting a bunch of summer flowers. It hadn't been the neatest of flower beds, but it had been bursting with color and looked really pretty. She left her dad and ran around to the kindergarten wing of the school. All of the flowers had been dug up, just as Mr. Jefferson had said! The bed was now just a bank of raked soil, and the flowers had vanished.

She saw Violet and Lexi and dashed over.

"Who would do such a thing?" she exclaimed.

"It's so mean!" said Lexi.

"I wonder if it was the same person who cut down Mr. Keating's ivy," said Mia. "Did you hear about that?"

"Yes," said Violet. "And the posters got ripped down, too. The weird thing is, look how clean the vandals left the flower bed. You'd think there'd be soil everywhere, but it looks like they've brushed it up and even raked it. They also took away all of the ivy leaves in Mr. Keating's yard. What vandals do that?"

"That is odd," said Lexi. She shook her head. "And what's also odd is that I woke up during the night with a weird feeling again."

"Spooky!" said Mia.

"Juniper said it might be...." Lexi broke off as the bell rang. "It doesn't matter."

"We'd better line up," said Violet. "We can talk more at lunch."

First period was canceled because Mrs. King called an emergency assembly. She told the children about the events of the night.

"This is very serious," she said. "Vandalism

is a crime. If anyone knows anything about what happened, I want you to tell a teacher. We must find out who did this. I really hope no one in this school is responsible."

Mia glanced at Nikhil, Josh, and Dan. They were looking as puzzled as everyone else. Despite Mr. Keating's words, she was sure it wasn't them. She'd known them all since preschool, and although they could be annoying, she'd never known them to vandalize anything, and she was sure they wouldn't do something that would upset the kindergarten children so much. She often saw them playing on the playground with their Book Buddies.

When they went back to their classrooms, Mia hurried into the girls' bathroom and shut herself in a stall. She'd had an idea. Pulling out her mirror, she whispered, "Show me last night when someone took the flowers from the flower bed."

She saw the flower bed, but then dark

shadows swirled across it. Her vision was being blocked by magic again!

"Show me Mr. Keating's ivy being cut down," she whispered.

But the shadows continued to swirl. Mia slowly lowered the mirror. So whoever had done the things during the night had been using magic just like the person the night before! Was it the same person? Surely there couldn't be two other people suddenly using magic in Westport! And why would they do helpful things one night and horrible things the next?

She remembered the kindergarten children crying because their garden had been ruined, and determination filled her. Whoever was doing these mean things was going to be sorry.

We'll find out who you are, she thought. *And we'll stop you!*

8
The Work of a Shade

After school, Mia and Sita went to Violet's house. Lexi persuaded her mom to let her join them after she'd finished her tennis lesson.

"I told her we're doing a project together," she said as they hurried down the road to the clearing. "It was the only way she'd let me come."

"It *is* a project, just not a school one," said Mia. "It's a magic one!"

They reached the clearing and called Bracken, Sorrel, Juniper, and Willow. Today there was no playing. They sat right down and told the animals what had been going on.

Sorrel hissed as Mia told them how she'd seen nothing but shadows when she had tried to find the culprits behind the night's activities. "We have to find out who's doing these things. I'm sure it's the same person, and I'll bet one of my whiskers that Shades are involved."

"It's strange that Lexi woke up feeling like something bad was happening during the night when it really was," said Sita.

"It was probably just a coincidence," said Lexi. "After all, I thought something horrible was happening two nights ago, but nothing bad was going on then."

Sorrel gave her a thoughtful look. "There are never coincidences when it comes to magic. I have a suspicion.... But no—" She broke off. "For now, I think we should focus on the mystery of what's been happening in town. We need to find out if Shades were behind these incidents."

"I've had an idea about that," said Violet. "Why don't I shadow-travel with Sita to the schoolyard, and then we can call you and Willow and see if you can smell any Shades near the flower bed?" Some Star Animals like Sorrel and Willow had the ability to smell when Shades had been around, causing bad things to happen.

"An excellent idea!" Sorrel purred.

"Let's go, Sita," said Violet. "All of the teachers will have gone home by now." She ran to a patch of shadows and held her hand out. Sita joined her, and as their fingers touched, both girls and their animals vanished.

"I wish we could have gone, too," said Lexi.

"I can watch what's happening using magic," said Mia. She took out her mirror. "Show me Sita and Violet!"

The surface swirled, and an image of the school playground appeared. Mia saw Violet and Sita suddenly appear in a patch of shadows beside the kindergarten wing and look around cautiously. A second later, Sorrel and Willow were there beside them. "They're at school," she said to Lexi. "Sorrel and Willow are sniffing around.... Oh!"

"What is it?" Lexi demanded.

"Sorrel's tail just puffed up, and Willow's ears have gone flat back," said Mia, frowning. Those weren't good signs.

"I wish I could see what you're seeing," said Lexi in frustration. "You three are all doing things to help and I'm not."

"Well, it's actually Sorrel and Willow who

are helping at the moment," Mia pointed out, watching in the mirror as the animals prowled around the schoolyard. "Violet and Sita aren't doing much."

Juniper looked at Lexi with his bright indigo eyes. "You might still develop other magic abilities, Lexi."

Bracken nodded. "Yes! Mia only just learned how to make shields, and Sita didn't realize she could command people at first."

"And even if you don't end up with any other powers, your magic is really good," said Mia.

"Not as good as everyone else's magic," Lexi muttered.

"It is," said Mia.

Lexi heaved a sigh.

"Is something wrong?" said Mia, putting the mirror

down and looking at her.

Lexi shrugged. "I guess it just sometimes feels like it's the three of you and then there's me. It's not your fault," she added quickly. "I know you didn't ask to have more magic than me, and I know I can't meet up as often as you three can because of all the extra things Mom makes me do, but sometimes.... Well, it feels like I'm on the outside, and you're all on the inside."

"But it's not like that at all!" exclaimed Mia. "Don't feel that way!"

"It's not just that, it's.... Oh, it doesn't matter." Lexi buried her face in Juniper's fur.

Before Mia could say anything else, Violet and Sita appeared back in the clearing and called Willow and Sorrel's names. The animals appeared, and they all raced toward Mia and Lexi. As they ran over, Mia had to push Lexi's strange words to the back of her mind. She would think about them later.

"It *was* a Shade!" hissed Sorrel. "A Shade destroyed the children's flower bed!"

"We could smell it really strongly," said Willow, shaking her head and snorting as if she wanted to clear her nostrils.

"That means there's definitely someone doing dark magic again!" said Bracken.

Violet nodded. "The question is—who? Who conjured the Shade?"

"And why?" said Mia, trying to get her thoughts together. "One night, things happen that are nice and helpful, like cutting the grass and painting the fence, and the next night, things happen that are horrible and mean. It makes no sense."

"We have to find where the Shade is," said Lexi.

"And what kind of Shade it is," added Juniper. "And who it's affecting."

"Do you think anything will happen tonight?" said Sita.

They exchanged uneasy looks—if it was a Shade, there was no way of knowing what it would do next!

In the morning, the girls woke up to disturbing news. Overnight, bicycles, scooters, slides, and jungle gyms had all vanished from people's yards. Children walked to school crying, with parents looking very upset.

Mia saw Lucia coming out of the house with Mr. Jefferson. He was comforting her. "Don't worry, sweetie. Nana and I will buy you another scooter," he was saying. He looked almost as upset as Lucia did. "Please don't cry."

"Today's a horrible day!" Lucia burst out. "My scooter's gone, and Nana's upset with me because one of her dolls' shoes is missing and she thinks I was playing with them without asking but I wasn't."

"It's all right. Don't worry," said Mr. Jefferson.

Mia's mom saw Sita's grandmother just ahead of them with Sita and Sita's baby brother, Arjun.

"Have you heard about the thefts? I can't believe people didn't see anything," Mrs. Greene said, catching up with her. "Surely thieves can't steal all of the play equipment in town and no one hear or see a thing!"

Thieves might not be able to, but a Shade could, Mia thought. She met Sita's eyes and could tell that she was thinking the same thing.

"Our neighbors had their grandson's slide stolen," said Sita's grandmother. "They thought they heard whispering in the yard during the night—in a foreign language, they said. But when they looked out of the window, there was no one there, and the slide was gone!"

Other people seemed to have similar stories. It was all anyone wanted to talk about. There were no tire tracks and no footprints, and nothing had been captured on any security cameras.

"What are we going to do?" said Mia to the others at lunchtime. They were sitting in a quiet spot on the playground.

"We have to find out where the Shade is," said Violet.

"Or Shades," said Sita. "It could be several of them, like when we fought the ones in the dreamcatchers and in the stretchy men."

"I can try searching with my magic, but I doubt it'll show anything," said Mia. She looked into her mirror. "Show me where the Shades are who have been doing all of the things in town!" she said hopefully.

But all she saw were shadows.

"Mia, a few days ago, you asked the magic to show you if there was anything we needed to investigate," said Lexi suddenly. "What did it show you? There might have been a clue in those images."

"You saw a TV remote, didn't you?" said Sita. "That was weird."

"Yes, I think so, and the road coming into town, a woman looking at herself in a mirror, and...." Mia frowned. "Yes, that was it. I saw some houses."

"Whose houses were they?" Lexi asked.

Mia thought back. "I'm not sure. One had ivy on it."

"Ivy? Like Mr. Keating's house—well, before all of the ivy was cut down?" said Violet quickly.

Mia caught her breath. Of course! That's why the ivy on Mr. Keating's house had looked familiar to her. "Yes! It *was* his house. I can't believe I didn't notice before!"

"Maybe the magic showed it to you because

Mr. Keating is the person behind all of this—maybe he's been conjuring a Shade," Lexi said.

"Mr. Keating?" Violet echoed. "I really can't imagine him doing dark magic."

"And he really wasn't happy about his ivy being cut down and his yard being cleaned up," said Sita.

"He also accused the boys,"said Mia. "Surely he wouldn't do that if he were responsible."

"Unless he wanted to trick people," Lexi pointed out.

They all considered it.

"I know how we can find out," said Violet suddenly. "Try to see him now, Mia. If he's the person doing dark magic, there'll be a blocking spell in place on him, so if you can't see him, we'll know he's guilty!"

"Good idea." Mia got out her mirror. "Show me Mr. Keating," she breathed.

An image of Mr. Keating immediately appeared. He was sitting in his living room, watching television.

"I can see him," she said as she saw him take a drink from a mug of tea. "So he can't be the person doing dark magic. He's watching TV."

"TV?" said Lexi suddenly. "The magic showed you a remote control, didn't it, Mia? Maybe there's a Shade in his TV!"

"No! It can't be that," said Mia, letting the magic fade. "We know whoever is doing magic is blocking me from seeing them. But I could see Mr. Keating and his TV just fine."

"Oh." Lexi's face fell. "I thought for a minute that we'd solved it."

"Not yet," said Mia, putting her mirror away. "But we will."

9
FINALLY, A CLUE!

"This is ridiculous!" Mia's dad declared as he and Mia stood and stared at the duck pond the next day. All of the ducks had been replaced by yellow plastic ones!

"Who could be doing these things?" said one of the other parents.

Mia stared in horror at the plastic ducks bobbing around in the pond. If a Shade was making real birds vanish, then things had gone way too far. She and the others had to figure this out.

"See you later, Dad!" she called, and breaking into a run, she sprinted for school. But as she did, she stepped on something. She stopped and picked it up. It was a small, oval piece of black plastic, slightly squashed at the sides. A memory stirred in Mia's head. She had seen something like this before. Yes, she'd found something similar by the baseball field the day after the fence had been painted. Was it just a coincidence?

There are never coincidences when it comes to magic. Sorrel's words echoed in her ears.

Mia had been about to put the piece of plastic in the garbage can, but now she hesitated. *Maybe it's a clue*, she thought, and she tucked it in her pocket instead.

"What do you think it is?" Violet said, turning the little piece of plastic over in her hands at recess.

"I have no idea," said Mia. "But don't you think it's odd that I found one at the pond and one at the baseball field?"

"Definitely," said Violet, handing it back. "And you know what else is odd? All of the streets were swept last night. There isn't a single scrap of litter to be found."

"What?" Mia stared at her.

"Yeah, I noticed on the way to school. I think everyone else has been so busy wondering what's going on with the ducks that they haven't realized that everywhere around town is looking really neat and clean."

"This is just too weird," said Lexi. "So we're looking for a Shade that sweeps the streets and swaps real ducks for plastic ones."

"A Shade that steals flowers and cuts ivy down, but who takes the leaves away and rakes the soil over afterward," said Sita. "What kind of Shade does that?"

"A crazy one," said Mia.

"I've been thinking—you know the houses you saw with magic?" said Lexi. Mia nodded. "Well, Mr. Keating's house might not have been the important thing in that image. Remember when some Shades had been put in dreamcatchers, and we were trying to figure out where they were? You saw the dreamcatchers in a vision, but you didn't realize the vision was showing you the dreamcatchers; you thought it was trying to show you the crystals on the shelf below."

"You're right," said Mia, nodding. "That's a really good point."

"So what else could you see when you saw Mr. Keating's house?" said Lexi.

"Mr. and Mrs. Jefferson's house next door," said Mia. "The street outside. That's it, I think, but I didn't get a very good look."

"Well, the Jeffersons can't be the ones conjuring Shades," said Sita. "Neither of them would ever do anything to harm the town or make the children unhappy."

Mia rubbed her forehead. She had a feeling that they were missing something important. "I'll try to see if I can find anything else out with my magic this evening. We're not meeting up, are we?"

"No. It's my brother's birthday, so I have to go right home," said Sita.

"I have a flute lesson," said Lexi.

"Mom wants me to go into town to get a new windbreaker," said Violet. "But starting tomorrow, it's spring break, and we'll have much more time to investigate. When I get home tonight, I might do some shadow-traveling with Sorrel to look around the outside of Mr. Keating's house, and the Jeffersons' place. I might find a clue, and I'll see if Sorrel can smell any Shades."

"Okay, but be careful," warned Sita. "Whatever you do, don't be seen!"

That evening, Mia lay on her bed, cuddling Bracken and thinking everything over. She'd tried asking the magic to show her where the Shade was and who'd been doing dark magic to conjure a Shade, but both times, all she'd seen were shadows again.

She ran over all of the different events in her mind—the helpful things and the mean things that had happened in town; the strange black plastic objects she'd found; and the images the magic had shown her—the houses, the woman, the remote control. She just didn't see how everything linked together.

"It's like there's something really important that we're missing or just not seeing," she said to Bracken. "If only we could figure out what type of Shade we're dealing with and what the person who conjured it wants to do."

Her phone buzzed. It was a message from Violet.

Just got back. Vxx

Mia texted back.

Did u find anything out? M

The next message came back almost in code. The Star Friends tried not to put anything about magic in their messages in case their parents or brothers and sisters picked up their phones and read them.

S could smell Ss near the houses. The smell was so strong that it made her sneeze! I didn't find any clues, though. Everything looked normal. I hope nothing else happens tonight. Vxx

Me, too. C u 2moro. Mx

Mia sighed as she put her phone down. The feeling that she was missing something was growing even stronger. Bracken nuzzled her.

"Oh, Bracken," Mia said, hugging him. "I just want to find out what's going on!"

That night, Mia had a nightmare again. She was standing in the middle of a dark room in a circle of light, and she could hear whispers coming from the shadows around her. Fear prickled across her skin. She sensed movement and swung around, but whoever it was had moved very fast. A memory stirred in her mind—an image of something moving quickly in one of her visions. The whispers grew louder, and she realized the people in the shadows were speaking in foreign languages.

"Come out!" she said bravely. "Stop hiding!"

There was a shifting movement in the shadows, and then all of the people stepped forward at the same time.

Mia gasped. They weren't people! They were Mrs. Jefferson's dolls, and their eyes were glowing red! The German doll was pointing his pitchfork at her; the Swiss milkmaid had her milk churn held threateningly over her head; the American cheerleader was holding her flag as if it were a javelin. The male Portuguese doll stepped forward, holding his wooden shepherd's crook like a weapon, and the female Portuguese doll raised her fists. Despite her fear, Mia noticed something looked different about her. What was it? Yes! Her black shoes were missing. But before she had time to think about that, the dolls started advancing on her.

"Bracken!" Mia screamed as the dolls leaped toward her.

She felt Bracken licking her face and woke with a start.

"I was having a nightmare!" she said,

pushing her hair back from her face. "It was horrible. It was about those dolls again."

"Two nightmares about the dolls." Bracken licked her face again. "This has to mean something, Mia. It has to be a magic dream. What were they doing?"

"They were attacking me," said Mia. She shivered and hugged Bracken close.

As she did so, her gaze fell on the two strange pieces of black plastic on her bedside table. The female Portuguese doll flashed into her head.

"Shoes!" she gasped suddenly. "The Portuguese doll didn't have shoes on." She grabbed the round plastic objects from her table. "I think that's because *these* are her shoes, Bracken!"

"But why would they be outside, by the duck pond and the baseball field?" asked Bracken.

Mia remembered what Mr. Keating and Sita's grandmother had said about hearing strange voices whispering in the night in foreign languages. Suddenly, the missing piece of the puzzle finally fell into place. "Because we're right—there isn't just one Shade," she said. "There are a bunch of them, and they're all trapped inside Mrs. Jefferson's dolls!"

10
Dolls and Shades

Mia wished she could shadow-travel like Violet or run as fast as Lexi so she could go to the others' houses to tell them what she'd found out, and they could figure out what to do next. But all she could do was send them a message saying she'd figured out where the Shades were and wait for them to wake up and check their phones in the morning.

At 7 a.m., her phone started buzzing like a bumblebee.

WHAT?!! Vxx

What do u mean u know where the Ss are? Lx

Where are they? Sxxx PS Are u okay?

Mia replied.

Yes, I'm okay. Just a little freaked out. I think they're in Mrs. Jefferson's dolls! I need u all to come over asap. Mx

Okay! I'll be there at 9! Vx

Me, too! Sx

Mia's heart sank when Lexi's message arrived a few minutes later.

I can't come! I have gymnastics, and Mom won't let me miss it. She said I can come over after, but don't wait for me. Mom just saw our neighbors out looking for their cat. It went missing in the night! That cd have something 2 do with the Ss, too. If you think u can find out what's going on, then just do it. U don't need me. Lx

Mia reread Lexi's last sentence, feeling torn. With everything that had been going on, she'd forgotten that she'd been planning to talk to Sita about Lexi. She really didn't want Lexi to feel any more left out, but if Lexi was right and cats were now missing, there was no time to waste.

She picked up her phone and typed a message.

> Okay, but make sure u come over as soon as u can. We DO need u! Mxxxx

She got dressed, her thoughts racing. Knowing the Shades were in the dolls was a big step forward. It meant that they knew where to find them so they could send them back to the Shadows. But they still had no idea what kind of Shades they were and who had been responsible for conjuring them and putting them in the dolls. Surely not Mr. or Mrs. Jefferson! No, Mia simply couldn't believe that. Someone else must have trapped them there for some reason, but how had that person done that—and when? Mrs. Jefferson had told Mia that she'd had the dolls since she was very young.

The unanswered questions raced around in Mia's head.

"You're quiet," her mom said as Mia sat at the table, barely able to eat even a mouthful of toast. "Are you feeling okay? I thought you'd be happy since it's the first day of spring break."

Mia shrugged. "I am. I just didn't sleep very well, and I'm not that hungry. The others are coming over soon. I'd better clean up my room."

She put the remains of her toast in the garbage can and hurried back upstairs.

At nine o'clock, Violet and Sita arrived. They rushed up to Mia's room. Shutting her door, they called their animals. It was risky, but Mia knew her sister Cleo wouldn't get up for a few more hours, and her dad had taken Alex out to the park. Her mom was busy downstairs doing some paperwork, so hopefully they wouldn't be disturbed, but just to be on the safe side, she put a chair behind the door to keep it closed.

"So what's going on?" Violet demanded, sitting on the rug with Sorrel. "What's this about the Shades being in the dolls?"

Mia quickly explained. "I'm sure Mrs. Jefferson's dolls have Shades in them," she said. "Sorrel, you smelled Shades outside the house, didn't you?"

Sorrel nodded. "Yes, it stank of them."

"So the dolls have been doing all of the stuff that's been going on at night—but why?" said Sita. "What kind of Shades are inside them?"

"I don't know," said Mia. She'd been thinking about it a lot, but she still hadn't figured it out. What Shades did both nice things, like painting the fence, and horrible things, like digging up a flower bed?

"Whatever they are, they have to be stopped today," said Sorrel.

"Yes. We need to go to Mrs. Jefferson's house this morning," said Violet. "Then we can send the Shades back to the Shadows."

Bracken leaped up. "Let's go!"

Mia's heart beat with a mixture of fear and excitement as she jumped to her feet, too. They were going to be fighting Shades again!

"Wait!" said Willow. "Is this wise? It sounds like there are a number of Shades if they're in all of the dolls."

"So? Sita can use her commanding magic to make them all freeze, and then I can order them to go back to the Shadows. It'll be easy," said Violet. Although Sita could command both people and Shades to do what she said, only Spirit Speakers like Violet could send Shades back to the Shadows. She had to be able to look them in the eye and then, when she commanded them, they would leave the human world.

"But how do we get to the dolls?" said Sita.

"We shadow-travel, of course! Come on!" Violet ran to a shadow next to Mia's wardrobe.

"Violet!" Sita protested. "We can't just appear in Mr. and Mrs. Jefferson's house. What if they're there and see us?"

"Sita's right," said Mia. "We've gotten into trouble before by rushing into things. I want to go in, too, but I think we should be careful."

Violet hesitated, and for a moment, Mia thought she might just go anyway, but then she sighed and stepped out of the shadows. "So what do you think we should do?"

"I think it might be best if we hang around near the Jeffersons' house and wait until we see them go out," said Mia. "Then we can shadow-travel inside and try to get to the dolls."

Violet looked disgruntled. "All right. We'll do things the slow way if we have to."

They walked to the Jeffersons' house. On the way, they saw a group of adults gathered around the town sign on the green. The flowers at its base had been replaced with artificial ones during the night.

"Why are the Shades doing these things?" Sita whispered.

"I have absolutely no idea," said Mia.

"To make people argue?" suggested Violet as they watched the grown-ups start to shout at each other.

"I guess it could be," said Mia. "The things they've done have made people upset."

"Painting the fence, sweeping the streets, and cutting the grass didn't," Sita pointed out.

"And the town does look really clean."

As they reached the Jeffersons' house, they saw Mrs. Jefferson coming down the path. "Oh, hello, girls!" she greeted them, but Mia noticed her smile wasn't as broad as usual. "You haven't seen a black-and-white cat, have you? My friend's cat disappeared during the night."

"Lexi's next-door neighbor's cat went missing last night, too," said Violet.

Mrs. Jefferson frowned. "I really don't know what's going on in town right now. Mike is beside himself. He's never known anything like this in all of the years he's lived here. It's making him sick."

"We'll keep our eyes peeled for the cats," said Mia.

"Thanks." Mrs. Jefferson hurried off.

"I wonder if Mr. Jefferson is out, too?" Violet whispered as Mrs. Jefferson disappeared around the corner.

"There's only one way to find out," said Mia.

She hurried up the path and knocked on the door.

There was a pause, and then it opened a little way. Mia saw Mr. Jefferson inside. "Oh, hello, Mia," he said, peering through the gap. He looked very stressed.

"I was just wondering if Lucia was here and wanted to play," Mia said.

"She's at home with her mom and dad," said Mr. Jefferson. "You could try there. Now I have to go." He quickly slammed the door. Mia frowned. She'd never known Mr. Jefferson to be so abrupt. She went slowly back to the others.

"Something's definitely going on," she said. "Mr. Jefferson was acting really oddly."

"Maybe he does have something to do with the Shades," said Violet.

They walked down the street and sat on a low wall near the stream, pretending to just be hanging out but really watching the Jeffersons' house. After a while, Mr. Jefferson came out, locked the door behind him, and hurried off.

"Now can we shadow-travel in?" said Violet eagerly.

Mia nodded. "All right."

"Let's text Lexi and tell her what we're doing first," said Sita. "Then when she gets home, she'll know where to find us."

"We could wait until she gets here before we go in," said Mia.

"But if we do that, the Jeffersons might come back," Violet pointed out. "This could be our only chance."

Mia knew she was right. Pulling out her

phone, she sent Lexi a quick message telling her they were at the Jeffersons' house and to meet them there.

They all stepped into a patch of shadows at the base of a willow tree.

Violet grabbed their hands. "Okay," she said, her eyes alight with excitement. "Here we go!"

11
The Heart's Desire Shades

Mia always found shadow-traveling a very strange experience. The world seemed to disappear around her, and for a moment, she had the feeling that she didn't weigh anything. Then her feet touched solid ground, and the world returned again. They were standing in the hallway on the other side of the front door in the Jeffersons' house. The door leading to the kitchen was open; the other doors—to the living room, study, and dining room—were shut.

The house should have been quiet, but

behind the dining room door, they could
hear the whispering of strange voices and the
sound of movement. The hairs on Mia's arms
prickled. Sita squeezed her hand tightly, her
eyes wide and scared. Even Violet looked
slightly alarmed.

Mia desperately wanted Bracken. She
whispered his name, and he appeared beside
her. She pressed her fingers to her lips,
warning him to stay quiet. He nodded and
pressed closer to her legs, his warm body
making her feel instantly braver.

A second later, Violet and Sita had followed her example, and Willow and Sorrel were there, too. Sorrel's fur puffed up as she sniffed the air, and Willow shook her head as if a bad smell were creeping up her nostrils.

"Shades?" Violet mouthed to Sorrel.

Sorrel nodded, her indigo eyes serious. She fixed her gaze on the dining-room door.

The hackles on Bracken's neck rose and he lowered his head, his lips curling back over his teeth as he stared at the door.

"We have to go in there!" Violet mouthed to the others, pointing to the door.

Sita started to shake her head.

Mia put her lips close to Sita's ear. "It'll be okay. Use your power as soon as we get in," she whispered as quietly as she could.

"On three," Violet mouthed. "One… two…three…." She leaped forward with Mia beside her, reaching for the door handle and pushing the door open.

"Now, Sita!" Mia cried, but as Sita burst into the room behind her, they all stopped in their tracks. The dolls were scattered around on the floor, lying on the rug as if they were just regular dolls that had been left there after someone had been playing with them.

Mia looked around slowly. What was going on?

"Shades!" hissed Sorrel. "This room reeks of them!"

Bracken snarled and leaped at one of the dolls, his jaws open, but before he could grab it, there was a flurry of inhumanly fast movement, and all of the dolls sprang to their feet. Mia squeaked in alarm as the dolls glared at them, their glassy eyes now glowing red, fists, milk churn, pitchfork, and flag raised.

"Whoever you are, you will not stop us!" said the American doll. "No one will stop us from granting a heart's desire!"

"We are Heart's Desire Shades, and we

make whatever is longed for come true," said the Irish doll. She gave a little giggle. "In our own special way, of course!"

The dolls edged closer, their red eyes full of malice. Bracken growled.

The German doll charged. Sorrel hissed and swiped at him with her claws. The doll spat out a word in German and slashed at her with his blunt pitchfork. With a yowl, she managed to leap out of the way just in time, but he was on her in a second, striking at her paws. Bracken snarled in fury and sprang at him, knocking him over. Willow was beside them in an instant, butting the doll hard with her head and sending him flying to the other side of the room, where he landed in a heap on the floor.

The other dolls drew in a collective gasp of fury.

Mia turned to Sita, who looked terrified. "Sita! Your magic!"

"F-freeze, dolls!" Sita gasped. Then her voice rose and grew more confident. "All of you! I command you to be quiet and stand still *right now*!"

The Irish and American dolls froze like statues. Only their red eyes flickered angrily from side to side. Mia felt a rush of relief, but it quickly changed to horror as she realized that none of the other dolls had frozen—they were all still moving!

"M-my magic's n-not working!" Sita stammered.

"It is, but only on two of the dolls!" Willow said, galloping over and lowering her head, preparing to protect Sita as the dolls surrounded them. Their voices rose, their different languages mixing together angrily.

"Try again, Sita!" Violet urged.

"Be quiet and stand still, dolls!" Sita shouted.

But her words had absolutely no effect. The girls and their animals were backed into a small circle at the center of the room; Bracken and Sorrel were growling and hissing; Willow was pawing angrily at the ground as the dolls advanced.

Mia opened herself to the magic current, pulling it inside herself just as the Portuguese doll lifted his wooden crook into the air. For a moment, Mia saw the other dolls' eyes flicker toward him as if they were waiting for a command. With a yell, he brought his crook down so that it pointed at the girls, and then he and all of the other dolls charged!

Shield! thought Mia. Instantly, a silvery bubble formed around and over her and the others. The dolls bounced off of its surface, yelling in shock as they hit the floor in a tangle of arms and legs. Mia concentrated on letting the magic flow through her as she heard Sita and Violet exclaim in relief.

"Oh, clever girl!" said Sorrel. "That was very quick thinking."

She felt Bracken nuzzle her hand. "You saved us, Mia!"

"For the moment. We can't stay in here forever," said Mia as the dolls got to their feet and started throwing things at the bubble—fruit from the Portuguese doll's basket, onions from around the French doll's neck, the flamenco dancer's castanets, and the milk churn.

"What are we going to do?" Sita cried as the German doll leaped at the bubble and started trying to stab it with his pitchfork, and the French doll attacked it with his baguette.

"I know!" breathed Violet suddenly, pressing her face to the side of the bubble so she could look into the German doll's eyes.

"Return to the Shadows!" she cried. "I am a Spirit Speaker, and I command you to return where you belong!"

Mia cheered and waited for the Shade to leave the doll and for the doll to fall lifeless to the floor, but it didn't. It just yelled furious words at her in German.

"Go back to the Shadows!" Violet shouted desperately.

But the doll didn't falter. He clearly didn't understand her. Mia's eyes widened as realization dawned.

"Why isn't my magic working?" exclaimed Violet.

"They must be using magic to help them block out your words and—" began Bracken.

"No," Mia interrupted Bracken. "It's not that! They can't be commanded because they don't understand English!"

While the dolls yelled and continued to attack the dome with anything that came to hand, everyone inside it fell silent.

"We need someone who speaks different languages," said Mia above the noise.

"Like me?" shouted a familiar voice.

"Lexi!" squealed Sita as Lexi pushed the window open and clambered in.

12
BEST FRIENDS FOREVER

Seeing Lexi, the dolls shouted angrily and
began to throw things at her, but Lexi was
using her magic, and she managed to dodge
and duck all of the flying objects. The German
doll charged at her, his pitchfork stretched out,
but Lexi was even faster. She raced to the other
side of the room in the blink of an eye.

"Lexi! We need to know the words for
freeze or *stand still and be quiet* in German,
French, Spanish, and Portuguese!" shouted
Mia. "Don't ask why. There isn't time!"

To her relief, Lexi didn't question her at all. "Um … in German, it's *Steht still und seid leise!*" she cried, dodging the pitchfork by jumping up on the dining table and then leaping right over the top of the silver dome to avoid the enraged French doll.

"*Steht still und seid leise!*" shouted Sita. The German and Swiss dolls stopped in their tracks, frozen in place. Lexi somersaulted over them.

Mia cheered. "What about French?" she cried.

"*Reste-là et tais-toi!*" said Lexi, landing and batting away an onion that was flying at her head. As Sita repeated the words, the French doll fell silent and froze.

There were just three dolls left—the Spanish flamenco dancer and the two Portuguese dolls. They surrounded Lexi. She tried to dodge, but the male doll shot behind her and kicked the back of her knees, making her fall over.

"I … er … don't know Portuguese," said Lexi, trying to scramble to her feet. "And I've only had one lesson of Spanish!"

The dolls saw her stumped expression and started to laugh, a sinister, evil sound that echoed around the room.

"Wait!" Violet pulled her phone out of her pocket. "We can find out!"

She started typing into the phone, but the dolls' eyes were gleaming wickedly. They leaped at Lexi, the female dolls jumping onto her back, yelling and yanking at her hair. Lexi cried out in pain.

Mia couldn't watch them attack Lexi and not do anything. She let the magic barrier disappear and charged forward. "Get off of her!" she shouted as Juniper sprang at the dolls, his little teeth bared and his paws outstretched. "Get off of her right now!"

The male doll slashed at Juniper with his crook. Bracken and Sorrel raced over, snarling and hissing.

"I've got it!" yelled Violet. "I don't know how to pronounce it, but I think be quiet and stand still in Spanish is … is …."

"¡*Quédate quieta y callada!*" shouted a deep voice. "And it's *Fiquem parados e quietos!* in Portuguese!"

Mia swung around. Mr. Jefferson was standing in the doorway.

"*¡Quédate quieta y callada!*" Sita pointed wildly at the dolls. "*Fiquem parados e quietos!*" All three dolls jerked to a halt, their red eyes glowing like fire.

"I knew it!" he said hoarsely, staring at them. "I knew there was something strange about those dolls. I told Ana I could hear them whispering every night this week, telling me they would grant my heart's desire. Ana didn't believe me, but I knew they were the ones doing things around town. I heard them moving at night!"

He looked at the girls, shock starting to register in his eyes. "What are you four doing here?" Mia tensed as he began to frown. "And where have these animals come from? Why are they—"

"Go to sleep, Mr. Jefferson!" Sita quickly commanded.

He blinked for a second as if he were going to argue, and then his eyes closed, and he sank to the floor.

"Good thinking, Sita!" said Mia, with relief.

"What's been going on?" demanded Lexi, looking around. "What's been happening?"

"Well…," Violet began.

"Wait!" Sita interrupted. "We need to send the Shades back to the Shadows first." She motioned to the dolls, standing like statues, their eyes burning with fury.

"Do your stuff, Violet," said Mia.

Violet walked up to the American doll, who was closest to her, and looked her straight in the eyes. "Return to the Shadows!" she commanded.

The doll's eyes glowed even more brightly for a second, and then the fire left them and she flopped down, a regular doll once again.

Violet put her back on the window ledge and then strode over to the Irish doll and repeated the words. The Shade left that doll, too.

"Now for the others," said Violet. "But we'll

need to find out how to say, 'Go back to the Shadows!' in the different languages."

"Guess this is where we really do have to use the Internet," said Lexi, pulling out her phone and typing into it. "Yes, here it is.... I have a translation app to help with my lessons. Here we go. Look at the French doll and say, *Retourne dans l'obscurité!*"

Violet did as she said, and the Shade vanished. One by one, the Shades were sent away until all of the dolls were back on the window ledge, their eyes glassy again instead of glowing red.

"No more Shades!" Violet exclaimed. "They're gone!"

Mia felt her breath leave in a rush. Bracken bounded around with Willow. Juniper scampered across the curtain rods in joy, and even Sorrel gave a delighted meow.

"So what's been going on?" Lexi demanded again.

They crowded around, telling her everything.

"But who trapped the Shades inside the dolls?" said Lexi. "And what type of Shades were they?"

"We don't know who yet," said Violet. "It couldn't have been Mr. Jefferson. Did you hear what he said? He knew there was something strange about the dolls. He wouldn't have said that if he'd been the one who'd put the Shades inside them."

"They told us they were Heart's Desire Shades," Sita told Lexi.

"They were using their magic to make Mr. Jefferson's heart's desire come true—

which I guess was for the town to win the competition," said Mia.

"Everything they did was about trying to make the town as clean as possible," said Violet. "But being Shades, they did that in ways that would upset people."

"I wonder what they did with the things they took—the scooters, the slides, the disappearing ducks, and the missing cats," said Lexi.

Mr. Jefferson mumbled something in his sleep. The girls looked at him. "We have to get out of here before Mrs. Jefferson gets home, but we can't just leave him on the floor asleep," Violet pointed out.

"We need to find out if he knows anything more and then make him forget all about seeing us and the Shades," said Mia.

"I can do that," said Sita. She glanced at the animals. "But maybe you'd better vanish first, just in case my magic doesn't stop him from forgetting about you."

Willow nuzzled her. "Good plan."

"We'll go straight to the clearing after we leave here and call you," Mia said to Bracken. He licked her hand and vanished.

Sita went over to Mr. Jefferson and crouched down beside him, gently touching his arm. Mia saw her breathe in and knew that she was connecting to the magic current. "You're going to wake up in a moment," she said to him. "And when you do, you will not be surprised that we're here. You're going to answer some questions, and when we leave, you'll forget everything about seeing us here and all about the dolls behaving strangely. Wake up now, Mr. Jefferson."

His eyes started to blink. Sita helped him sit up. Mia wondered what he would say when he caught sight of them, but Sita's magic worked perfectly. He didn't seem surprised to see them and instead just smiled. "Hello, girls. Goodness, what am I doing down here?"

"You just tripped," Sita said, helping him to his feet. "Up you go."

Mr. Jefferson's eyes widened. "The dolls...." He broke off as he caught sight of them on the window ledge. "I must be coming down with something. You know, I thought the dolls were alive and there were four wild animals in this room." He shook his head. "Those dolls. All this last week, I've been thinking I can hear them talking to me, telling me they'd grant my heart's desire. Then I started hearing strange animal noises from the equipment shed near the baseball field this morning. I'd just come back to get the key to go and find out what was inside." A worried look crossed his face. "I think I'd better see a doctor."

"No. There's no need to see a doctor," Sita said. "Do you understand?"

Mr. Jefferson nodded obediently. "No doctor," he repeated.

"And you don't need to worry about the dolls. They're just dolls."

He nodded again. "Just dolls."

"Do you have the key to the shed?" Violet asked suddenly.

Mr. Jefferson went over to the table and took a key out of a little bowl.

Sita smiled. "Good. Please give that to Violet, and then come and sit down in the living room and take a nap." She took him by the arm and led him to the living room. "Sit down and shut your eyes. When you wake up, you will have forgotten all about seeing us and the strange noises and talking dolls."

Mr. Jefferson sat down and shut his eyes.

"Sleep now," Sita told him, and he started to gently snore.

The girls looked at each other. "Strange animal noises in the shed?" said Violet, holding up the key. "I think this is something we need to investigate. Time to shadow-travel again!"

She stepped into a patch of shadows by the TV and held out her hands. They all linked fingers, and then Mia felt the world fall away.

Her feet landed on grass. She opened her eyes to see they were now standing in the shadows behind the equipment shed. It was a very large shed in the corner of the baseball field where all of the sports equipment was stored. A faint quacking was coming from inside.

"Ducks!" she exclaimed.

Violet ran around to the front of the shed. She turned the key in the lock and opened the door. In the dim light, they could see slides, scooters, bikes, and a group of ducks staring at them with surprised dark eyes. They quacked loudly and waddled toward the open doorway.

"This must be where the dolls put everything!" Mia realized.

The ducks came out into the fresh air, flapped their wings, and flew off in the direction of the duck pond.

From the back of the shed, the girls could hear the sound of scratching coming from a large cupboard. Lexi ran over and opened it. Two cats sprang out, looking rumpled and cranky. They raced for the door and disappeared across the baseball field.

"Poor cats," said Violet. "At least they weren't in here for too long."

"What should we do about all of the scooters and bikes?" Lexi said.

"I vote we just leave them here," said Mia. "We can't return everything without people noticing. So if we leave the stuff here, everyone will find it and think it was someone playing a silly prank."

"Good plan," said Violet. "Let's go to the clearing."

Leaving the shed door open, they shadow-traveled to the shadows in the trees at the side of the clearing. But when they got there, they saw Mary from the Copper Kettle sitting on a tree stump.

"How about the beach instead?" whispered Lexi.

They nodded and hurried through the trees and out onto the clifftop. A brisk breeze was blowing, and white clouds were scudding across the sun. The girls ran across the windswept grass to the stony path that led down the cliff to the beach. It was deserted. The tide was just starting to go out, the waves pulling back on the pebbles, leaving them shining and damp. The girls headed along the narrow strips of sand to their secret place. Squeezing in between the rocks, they called their animals' names.

The Star Animals appeared right away. "So, what happened?" demanded Bracken.

"Did you deal with the man?" said Sorrel.

"Did your magic work?" Willow asked Sita.

"Yes," Sita said.

"Brilliantly!" Mia added.

They told the animals everything.

"One thing I still don't get is how you suddenly appeared, Lexi," said Violet.

"I was just getting in from gymnastics when I read Mia's text, and at the same time, I got one of my horrible feelings, but it was worse than all of the others I've had. It made me feel really worried. I tried to text you back, Mia, but you didn't reply. I knew that was odd because you almost always reply right away, so I decided to use my magic to run to the Jeffersons' house. I was taking a look around the house to see if I could find you when I heard voices coming from the open window. I peeked in and saw what was happening...."

"And then saved the day," Sita finished.

Mia hugged Lexi. "Thank you!"

"I don't know why I had such a strong feeling that something was wrong," said Lexi. "But I'm glad I did."

"I believe you're developing a new power, Lexi," said Sorrel, fixing her with a thoughtful

look. "I believe you're developing the ability
to sense when dark magic is threatening people
nearby."

"I agree with Sorrel," said Juniper. "I told
you I thought something like that might be
happening."

"I know, but I didn't quite believe it."
A smile lit up Lexi's face. "This is awesome!
With a power like that, I'll be able to really
help fight dark magic."

"You help already," Mia told her quickly. "Your agility magic is amazing. If it hadn't been for that, you wouldn't have gotten to us in time...."

"You wouldn't have been able to climb in through the window so quickly," said Sita. "Or dodge the dolls."

"And it's not just your magic that we need," said Violet. "We need your brain. None of us knew the foreign words to stop the dolls."

"And you were the one who realized that, although I thought the magic was showing me an image of Mr. Keating's house, it could be that we were supposed to be looking at something else in the image. I should have been looking at Mr. and Mrs. Jefferson's house," Mia reminded Lexi. She hugged her. "You're amazing in so many ways. We couldn't possibly manage without you!"

Lexi glanced around tentatively. "So, when

I'm not at the same school as you next year, you won't need me anymore and that the three of you will want to be Star Friends without me?"

They stared at her.

"Of course not!"

"No way!"

"Why would you think that?"

Lexi looked a little embarrassed and picked at a fingernail. "I don't know. It's just that I've been thinking about how we're going to be at different schools and how weird that'll be," she admitted. "Everything's going to change."

Sita took her hand. "It will be strange being at different schools, but we'll always be best friends."

"Always," said Mia. "That won't ever change."

It was as if a heavy weight that had been sitting on Lexi's shoulders were now suddenly lifted. Her eyes shone as she looked at her friends. "I've been so worried about it!"

Violet frowned. "Lexi, for someone who's really smart, you can be really silly at times. We're best friends, and that's that."

Lexi smiled. "So, what do we do next?"

"Well, first we need to figure out who put those Shades in the dolls," Violet said.

"And we have to figure out why the magic showed a picture of a woman looking in a mirror, and a TV remote," said Mia. "They may be important clues." She glanced up. The clouds had cleared from the sky, and the sun was shining down. "But we have all of spring break to work on that. Right now, I think we should have some fun! I want ice cream, but first—who wants to swim?"

"Me!" they all said, except for Sorrel.

Mia pulled off her socks and shoes and squeezed out between the boulders. The beach was still deserted. She ran toward the water, her feet sinking into the soft sand.

Bracken yapped and bounded past her to the water's edge. Juniper and Willow quickly followed with the girls, while Sorrel picked her way very cautiously across the wet stones, stopping every now and then to shake a paw.

Bracken leaped into the water, jumping around with Willow, while Juniper scampered at the edge of the waves and Sorrel stood back a bit. The other girls rolled up their jeans and waded into the water, too.

"Come and play, cat," Bracken said, bounding out toward Sorrel.

She arched her back. "You're wet! Stay back!"

Bracken shook himself, covering her with water droplets.

She hissed and leaped back. "I'll get you for that, fox!"

"Have to catch me first," Bracken said playfully.

Violet grinned and ran over to pick Sorrel up. "Don't worry about him, Sorrel," she said. Looking slightly happier, Sorrel purred and cuddled up in Violet's arms.

"Isn't this wonderful?" said Lexi, turning her face upward. "I love the sunshine."

"I love vacation!" said Sita happily, linking arms with Lexi. "Beach trips, ice cream, seeing friends, and…"

"Having exciting magical adventures!" finished Mia. She spun around in the water, happiness filling her as she watched Bracken, Willow, and Juniper playing in the sparkling waves while her friends laughed, their faces lit up by the golden rays of the sun.